The KING of KINDERGARTEN

DERRICK BARNES

ILLUSTRATED BY
VANESSA BRANTLEY-NEWTON

NANCY PAULSEN BOOKS

hat if   the sky   should

NANCY PAULSEN BOOKS

an imprint of Penguin Random House LLC, New York

Nancy Paulsen Books is a registered trademark of Penguin Random House LLC.

Visit us online at penguinrandomhouse.com

Library of Congress Cataloging-in-Publication Data

Names: Barnes, Derrick D., author. | Brantley-Newton, Vanessa, illustrator.

Title: The King of Kindergarten / Derrick Barnes; illustrated by Vanessa Brantley-Newton.

Description: New York, NY: Nancy Paulsen Books, an imprint of Penguin Random House LLC, [2019]

Summary: Instilled with confidence by his parents, a young boy has a great first day of kindergarten.

Identifiers: LCCN 2018022832 | ISBN 9781524740740 (hardcover: alk. paper) | ISBN 9781524740757 (ebook) | ISBN 9781524740771 (ebook)

Subjects: | CYAC: First day of school—Fiction. | Kindergarten—Fiction. | Schools—Fiction. | Self-confidence—Fiction.

Classification: LCC PZ7.B26154 Kin 2019 | DDC [E]—dc23

LC record available at https://lccn.loc.gov/2018022832

Manufactured in China by RR Donnelley Asia Printing Solutions Ltd.

ISBN 9781524740740

10   9   8   7   6   5   4   3   2

Design by Eileen Savage. Text set in Carter Sans Pro.

The artwork was hand drawn and then colored using Adobe Photoshop and Corel Painter.

TO PRINCE NNAMDI THELONIUS—MY BABY. —D.B.

FOR ALL THE CHILDREN OF THE WORLD, I SEE YOU. —V.B.-N.

A child must learn early to believe that he is
somebody worthwhile and that he can do
many praiseworthy things. The child must
have the love of family and the protection they
give in order to LIVE and FLOURISH.

—Benjamin Mays

THE MORNING SUN blares through your window like a million brass trumpets.

It sits and shines behind your head— like a crown.

Mommy says that today, you are going to be the King of Kindergarten!

You'll use a golden brush to clean Ye Royal Chiclets.

You'll wash your own face with a cloth bearing the family crest.

You'll dress yourself neatly in handpicked garments from the far-off villages of Osh and Kosh. *B'gosh!* You'll be ready to reign!

"My baby is heading to school," Mommy will say during breakfast.

But you're not a "baby"—could a baby wolf down a tower of pancakes the way you can?

I don't think so.

"You're growing up so fast," Daddy will say. And he'll be right!

"I can't stay the same size forever, can I?" you'll say. "One day, I'll be taller than you, Daddy, and you'll be my li'l man."

Daddy will laugh, but you won't be joking.

Then a big yellow carriage will
deliver you to a grand fortress.

SCHOOL BUS

As you walk up to the towering doors, you'll remember Mommy saying, "Hold your head high and greet everyone with a brilliant, beaming, majestic smile. For you are the King of Kindergarten."

Your teacher will welcome you with a warm smile and a friendly "Good morning."

She'll be delighted by how you recite your name with pride.

When you head to your royal seat, the kids at your round table will wave and say "Hi!" like they've been waiting on you all summer.

So you smile back, return the wave, and give them a cheerful "Hi, everybody!"

The truth is, you couldn't wait to meet your Kindergarten Kingdom, either.

Your teacher will go over classroom rules, and you'll all discuss important matters such as shapes, the alphabet, and the never-ending mystery of numbers. She'll even read a book about trucks, trains, and tractors.

WHEW! It sounds like a lot, but you're the King of Kindergarten. Piece. Of. Cake.

You will show your bravery at recess when you go up to one of your classmates and ask, "Marie, do you wanna play with me?"

Not only will she say yes, but she'll lead
the way in helping you save the kingdom by
battling a fire-breathing dragon!

In the cafeteria, the boy sitting next to you will be missing dessert.

You'll have packed your favorite—chocolate pudding—with an extra cup just in case.

So you'll say to him, "Want a pudding, Howie?"

He'll say thanks, and you won't mind at all, because what could be cooler than sharing with new friends?

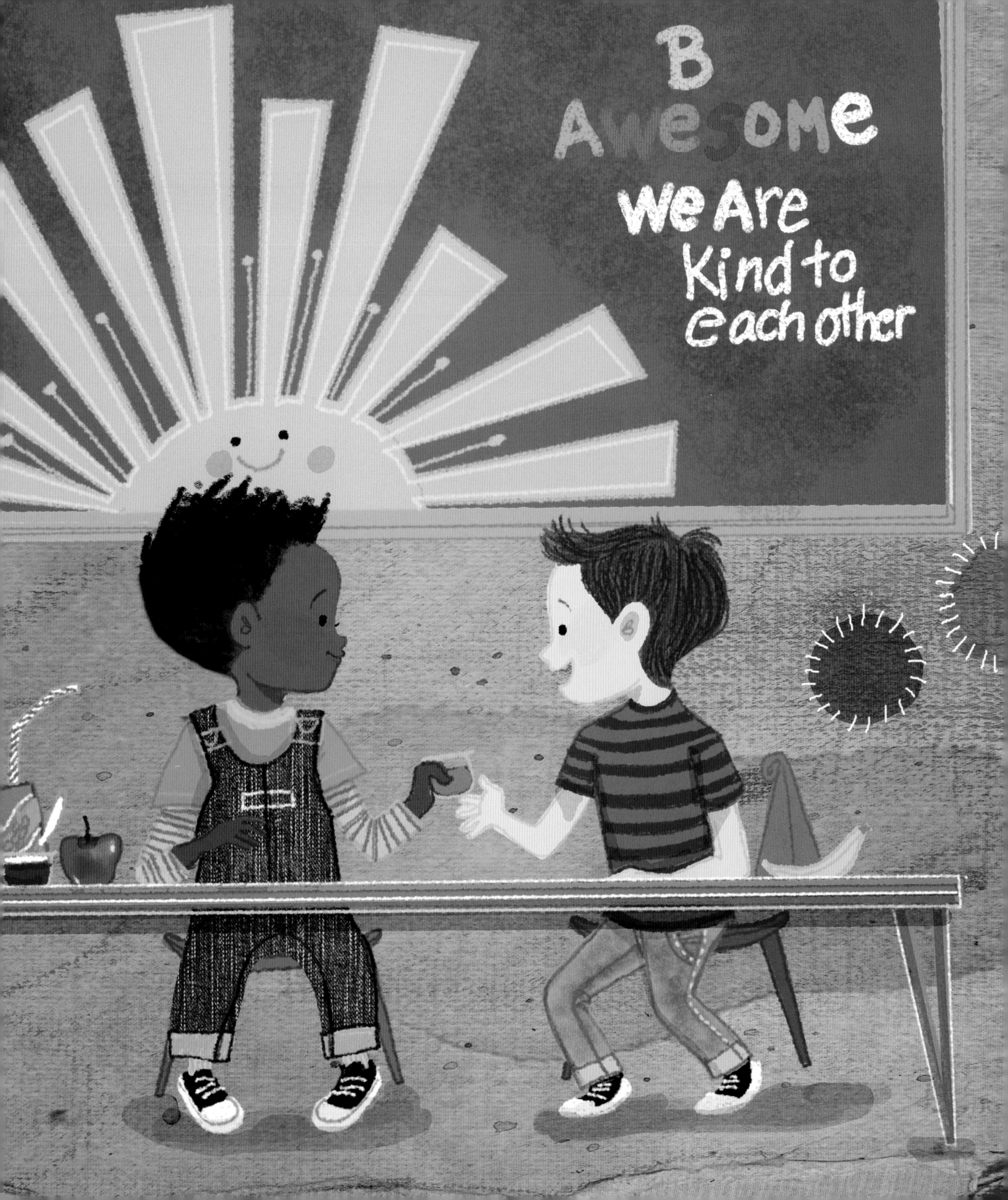
B AWESOME
We Are Kind to each other

After a royal rest,

you'll arise to sing and dance
and bop to a rhythmic beat.

The day will be one you'll never forget.

At the end of it, your teacher will wish you all a magnificent evening and bid you farewell until dawn.

On your way back home, you'll think of all the things you can't wait to tell your parents. "I made a bunch of new friends. My teacher is nice. And recess is the best thing ever!"

And tomorrow, it will begin again—another day as
the charming, the wonderful, and the kind . . .

King of Kindergarten.